TANGLED
FORTUNES

ALSO BY MARGARET MAHY:

Published by Delacorte Press

The Door in the Air and Other Stories

THE COUSINS QUARTET
The Good Fortunes Gang
A Fortunate Name
A Fortune Branches Out
Tangled Fortunes

BOOK FOUR OF

THE COUSINS QUARTET

TANGLED FORTUNES

MARGARET MAHY

ILLUSTRATED BY
MARIAN YOUNG

DELACORTE PRESS

J
MAH

Published by
Delacorte Press
Bantam Doubleday Dell Publishing Group, Inc.
1540 Broadway
New York, New York 10036

A Vanessa Hamilton Book

Book design by Claire N. Vaccaro

Library of Congress Cataloging in Publication Data
Mahy, Margaret.
Tangled fortunes / by Margaret Mahy ; illustrated by Marian Young.
p.   cm. — (The Cousins quartet ; bk. 4)
Summary: The relationship between Tracey Fortune and her brother
Jackson is temporarily strained by Tracey's desire to be a
bridesmaid in her cousin's wedding and by the mysterious messages
that Jackson begins to receive.
ISBN 0-385-32066-3
[1. Brothers and sisters—Fiction.   2. Cousins—Fiction.   3. New
Zealand—Fiction.]   I. Young, Marian, ill.   II. Title.
III. Series: Mahy, Margaret. Cousins quartet ; bk. 4.
PZ7.M2773Tan   1994
[Fic]—dc20   93-32202
                                                           CIP
                                                           AC

Manufactured in the United States of America

November 1994

10   9   8   7   6   5   4   3   2   1

TO
ALICE, LUKE, JACK,
NELLIE, ARTHUR, AND GILES

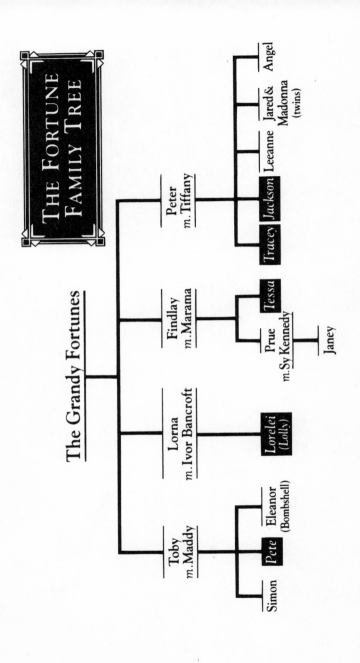

The Grandy Fortunes

THE FORTUNE FAMILY TREE

Toby m.Maddy — Lorna m.Ivor Bancroft — Findlay m.Marama — Peter m.Tiffany

Simon — Pete — Eleanor (Bombshell)

Loreli (Lolly)

Prue m.Sy Kennedy — Tessa

Janey

Tracey — Jackson — Leeanne — Jared & Madonna (twins) — Angel

CHAPTER 1

Just as Jackson and his big sister, Tracey, were about to leave for school, the phone rang. Tracey was right beside it, but she didn't answer. She always made Jackson do the things she couldn't be bothered with.

"You get that!" she cried, pretending she had left something in her bedroom that she had to find at once.

Jackson, however, enjoyed answering the phone, and always tried to make himself sound fascinating to the unknown person at the other end.

"Excellent-Jack-sharp-as-a-tack," he announced.

"Answer the phone properly, Jackson," his mother, Tiffany, yelled from the kitchen. "Don't confuse people." The response, though, when it came, was more confusing than anything Jackson had ever said—a whispering of a jumpy word that Jackson couldn't quite hear.

"What?"

The voice stopped whispering, and muttered instead.

"Owangabangabootabotta!" Or that was what it sounded like.

"Say it slowly, man," cried Jackson.

His younger sister, Leeanne, rushed past him, putting on her backpack as she ran. She was holding a Barbie doll in her teeth, just as pirates in old pictures used to be shown holding knives.

"Jackson, did you change that grubby T-shirt?" called his mother. Jackson could hear the baby howling, while the twins, who were four, rode the family tricycle around and around the table. No, he had not changed his T-shirt. It was his favorite one—black, with a polo neck—and it went wonderfully well with his sunglasses. Jackson studied the shirt. Perfectly clean, he thought, except for a smear or two that no one would notice unless they peered at him closely. He certainly didn't want to keep Tracey waiting when she was in such an impatient mood.

"Bye, Mom," he yelled, and shot out onto the porch, slamming the door behind him so that he would be able to pretend he hadn't heard her call.

Tracey was waiting for him.

"Let's rock and roll, man!" Jackson cried, pulling his sunglasses down from his forehead to hide his eyes. Blue eyes, he reckoned, looked wrong for a heavy-metal rock star.

"We're late, ratbag, and it's all your fault," Tracey grumbled, setting off on her skateboard. Jackson fell in behind her, just as he had always done. Yet these days, he often found himself thinking it would be fun to set off first and lead the way, just for a change. Wouldn't it be great, he thought, to look ahead and see space—rather than Tracey's back and shoulders, tough and knobbly under her blue shirt. "Watch out, world! Here I come!" he would shout to the open air.

The family dog, a strange-looking woolly animal, watched them go. His mother had been the next-door dog, mostly Labrador, but his father was a poodle from Fairfield Hill—the rich part of town. He looked more like a long-legged mischievous black sheep than a dog, and he had no real name. Everyone called him the Labradoodle. He stood beside the gate wearing his most noble expression, wagging his tail as if it

magician casting a spell.

"Somebody called up a

gabootabotta'!" Jackson cried,

time to the word. When he wa

anything he always turned to drum

"Some weirdo!" said Tracey. "You

have me, Jackson, or you'd turn into

yourself."

It was typical of Tracey to believe her

strangeness was the only acceptable kind. Perha

it would be nice to try another sort of strangeness,

Jackson thought. Perhaps it would be nice to have

friends, even if Tracey did not approve of them.

On the other hand, how could he desert Tracey?

She might have the occasional bad-tempered day.

But she had looked after him since before he could

remember, and he knew she would never desert

him.

were a wand and he were

nd said, 'Owangaban-
clapping softly in
ted to remember
beats.
're lucky to
a weirdo

own
ps

,, and Leeanne set out
more or less the same time. But Jackson and Tracey always pushed ahead of Leeanne.
They wanted to travel by skateboard, and she pre-
ferred to go to school with her friend, Katherine
Burns, who collected Barbie dolls, just as Leeanne
did. As they walked, they shook their Barbie dolls
in the air, making Barbie-doll conversation in
squeaky voices.

Jackson and Tracey glided down a gently sloping sidewalk, leaving Leeanne to find her own way
to school. Navigating around the crowd at a bus
stop, they flowed on to the corner of Main Road.
This ran, straight and true, past some shops to an

intersection with Bright Street where their cousins, Tessa and her grown-up sister, Prue, lived.

"There's Tessa waiting for us," said Tracey. "She probably wants to boast about being a bridesmaid all over again."

"Ba-a-a-ad deal!" bleated Jackson. "Bridesmaids! Yuk! Shall we cut all bridesmaids out of the gang?"

Tracey shrugged. "Better not," she said. "We'd lose two members."

Tracey and Jackson, along with Tessa and two other cousins, Lorelei and Pete, were members of a secret gang called the Good Fortunes Gang (though Tessa sometimes tried to make it seem more official by calling it an Investment Society). Leeanne was not a member of the Good Fortunes Gang. Everyone in the gang had agreed that nobody who collected Barbie dolls could belong. Leeanne didn't seem to mind. She and Katherine and one or two other girls had their own Barbie-Doll Club, and wrote flowery little letters from one doll to another.

In the distance, under the green summer umbrella of the Bright Street corner tree, Tessa waited for them, leaning on her bicycle and glancing every now and then at her digital stopwatch—a free gift to new subscribers to *Time* magazine.

"All clear! Let's motor," said Tracey, speeding up.

Main Road was busy, but the sidewalk was almost empty, and there was no one around who might telephone the school complaining about skateboarders on the sidewalk. Jackson loved the rush of summer air on his face, and the feeling that, at any moment, he might rise, skateboard and all, and fly over the roofs of Fairfield. If he had been on his own, without Tracey in front of him, he felt he might actually have taken off.

"Wheeee!" he cried softly.

"Shut up!" said Tracey. "The antiskateboard crowd will notice us."

Together they swept up to the Bright Street corner, Tessa, and the tree.

"Hi!" yelled Tracey, spinning around in front of Tessa with supreme skill. Watching her spin as though she wasn't even thinking about it, Jackson felt proud to be Tracey's brother. She had spent many years scraped and bruised, but now she almost never fell.

"Hi!" Tessa cried, taking no notice of Tracey's skillful performance. "Forty-two seconds late.

Come on, or we'll miss first bell." She liked to be at school in time to arrange things in her desk so that it looked like the desk of a busy executive vice-president. She had a desk calendar and a sign that said WHEN THE GOING GETS TOUGH, THE TOUGH GET GOING.

"Why were you waiting for us?" asked Tracey.

"Yeah, man, what's coming down?" echoed Jackson. Tessa looked secretive and important.

"I'm calling an extraspecial gang meeting this afternoon," Tessa said. "I'll tell you everything then."

"Tell us now!" demanded Tracey, sounding irritated with whatever it was before she even knew anything about it.

"Something *funny* is going on, and nobody at home believes me," Tessa said, looking back over her shoulder. At that moment a motorcycle engine exploded into life, and the motorcycle roared away down Bright Street.

"Take a note of that!" Tessa cried in a low, urgent voice. "Then you can give evidence later."

"He was riding a Norton," said Tracey, peering after the motorcyclist.

"Just remember his red helmet," said Tessa mysteriously, "and remember that, right this moment, our house is filling up with wedding presents."

Jackson groaned loudly at the mention of the wedding.

Tessa's sister, Prue, was about to marry Christopher Moody. He was the son of a city council member who lived on Fairfield Hill, the rich part of town. Jackson couldn't make out why there was so much fuss over this wedding. It wasn't as if Prue were getting married for the first time. She'd done it all once before. She even had a baby named Janey. Still, for weeks, family conversation had been all about the wedding. Tessa and Lorelei were to be bridesmaids, and there was going to be a big party.

Jackson loved the idea of a party as much as anyone, but he was bored with all the talk about bridesmaids' dresses. He was glad that Tracey was much too tough, tall, knobbly, and adventurous to think about being a bridesmaid. Mind you, thought Jackson uneasily, it was odd the way she sometimes seemed to talk more about bridesmaids than Tessa did.

"This engagement's a real pain," grumbled Tessa. "I don't even want to be a bridesmaid!" She and Tracey moved ahead of Jackson. Now there were two backs for him to follow.

"You wouldn't like it, though, if nobody had asked you to be one," said Tracey.

"But I'm going to have to wear a pink dress with frills," said Tessa. "And all people who are good at business, like executive vice-presidents, hate frills."

"I read in a magazine that frills look okay if the person wearing them is tall," said Tracey. "Short people don't look good in frills, but tall ones do. And I think Prue should have more than two bridesmaids."

Tessa looked at her in surprise.

"I mean, two's not very many," Tracey said. "If you're having a big wedding, you should have a whole *team* of bridesmaids. And you ought to have someone from each family."

"Owangabangabootabotta!" muttered Jackson to himself. It didn't sound like a dictionary word. And who had muttered it at the other end of the phone?

As they turned a corner, the school gates came into view.

"Hi, Jackson!" someone cried.

"How's it coming down, man?" Jackson

shouted back, sounding friendly. Tracey forgot about bridesmaids and spun around sharply, nearly knocking Tessa over on her bicycle.

Biking past them was a boy named Oakley Flangrove, one of those awkward-looking kids, his front teeth too big for the rest of his face. He was well known for being weird, not only because of his name, but because he took ballet lessons. He was also the great violin star of the class music group, whereas Jackson merely shook a tambourine. Oakley was a school librarian as well, and answered lots of questions in class, almost as if he were sucking up to the teacher. Yet Jackson liked Oakley, without knowing why. It was a pity that Tracey disapproved of him so strongly.

"Don't wave at Oakley Flangrove," she ordered. For once Jackson was a little rebellious.

"Why not?" he asked. "Oakley's okay! He's got rhythm, man."

"He has *not* got rhythm. He's weird," Tracey snapped. "You don't want to go around with anyone weird, do you? And he's related to the Kennedys, and they insulted us." Jackson thought she had finished, but then she added, "And stop calling me 'man.'"

Though Jackson's cousin, Prue, the bride-to-be, called herself Prue Fortune, her official name was Prue Kennedy. Her first husband was Sy Kennedy, Oakley Flangrove's uncle. If Prue had stayed married to Sy, Oakley might have been a sort of cousin-by-marriage, and then Jackson would have been allowed to go around with him. But Sy Kennedy had run away to Australia, leaving Prue all alone with a baby when she was only eighteen. Thank goodness, everyone said, that she had a family to come home to! What a relief it must have been to be a Fortune again.

By now they were almost at the school. In the distance Jackson could see another cousin, Pete Fortune, walking toward the school. Seeing them, Pete lifted his arms in the air and clapped his hands twice above his head. It was a Good Fortunes Gang sign. Jackson signaled back to Pete, dancing a little on his skateboard as he clapped. Tessa and Tracey could not be bothered to signal.

"Why doesn't Prue ask Pete to be a bridesmaid?" Tracey asked, making a joke of the bridesmaid business.

Tessa laughed heartily. "Great idea!" she said. "And Prue's into that nonsexist stuff too." Then she stopped laughing and sighed. "You're lucky, Trace. At least you're one hundred percent safe from the pink-frilly-dress doom."

"Yeah! Suppose so," said Tracey, but she did not sound as pleased as Jackson thought she would be.

"Gang meeting after school," Tessa shouted to Pete. "Don't miss it. I'm going to tell about the mysterious prowler."

The bell rang loudly, and all four began to run across the playground.

"What prowler?" Pete asked Jackson as they ran, but Jackson did not know.

When he finally collapsed at his desk, panting like the Labradoodle, Jackson saw that there was an envelope waiting for him. A single word was written on it. *Owangabangabootabotta*. He had the beat of it in his head, so he had no trouble recognizing it in print. The teacher was just walking through the door as he opened the envelope.

> *Bam bam bombinate*
> *Tattoo, tap, and tan.*
> *Quodlibet! Quodlibet!*
> *Ran dan dan!*

Every line was written in a different color. Under the lines there was a drawing of an egg in an eggcup. Two clues in one morning!

Jackson slumped down in a dream, half expecting to hear Tracey say, "Give me that!" and to feel the paper whisked from between his fingers. But Tracey was two classes away. Here was a mystery that was all his own. It was almost as good as skateboarding down a smooth, open, slightly downhill sidewalk with nobody in front of him, nobody shouting instructions at him, or telling him where to go.

CHAPTER 3

"Owangabangabootabotta!" said Jackson. "Quodlibet! Quodlibet! Ran dan dan!" He was saying the words aloud to himself, thinking that the sound of them might tell him what they meant. He couldn't help tapping the beat out with his ballpoint pen.

"*Quod*libet! *Quod*libet!"

"Jackson, you're tapping again!" said Miss Hood in a tired voice. She was always telling him not to tap or jiggle. "And that reminds me, will the music group meet in the library at recess? We need to run through our piece for the school concert."

Jackson couldn't help tapping and jiggling. After all, it was a tapping, jiggling world. All sorts of things had a hidden beat to Jackson and he wanted to join in with a beat of his own. He quite looked forward to practicing with the music group so that he could do a little bit of legal rattling.

The music group was made up of ten recorder players and a few extras. The teacher played the piano, and Oakley Flangrove played the violin. Jackson liked to think of himself as the drummer, but they did not have a set of drums, so he had to make do with a tambourine in most pieces, and two maracas in a song that was supposed to come from Brazil.

"There's no need to wriggle quite so much, Jackson," said Miss Hood. "Just stand nice and straight and shake the maracas in the way that I showed you. And now we'll do 'Greensleeves.' " The recorders began their piping—one recorder a little bit behind all the others.

"Stop!" called Miss Hood. "Let's all try to start together this time, shall we?"

There was not a lot for a drummer to do during "Greensleeves." Jackson shook the tambourine softly. But as he did so the old song took on a new, hot rhythm in his mind. He dreamed of a set of drums right there in front of him. In his dream *he* was in charge of the drums. Jackson rattled the tambourine and twisted a little in time to the sprightly "Greensleeves" in his head. It wasn't coming in at his ears but seemed to begin somewhere between his ribs, and go right through him in every direction.

"Boogie on down, man!" he said, and then realized he had spoken aloud in his jazz voice—a hoarse, deep voice he only used when drumming. "Greensleeves" wailed, recorder by recorder, into silence.

"Did you say something, Jackson?" asked Miss Hood.

"Nothing much," Jackson said hastily. "I was being a jazzman. I was improvising."

"Jackson, you are not to improvise," said Miss Hood. "And you are not a jazzman."

Jackson tried to explain. "I can't help it sometimes," he said.

"Jackson, if you can't help it we might have to get someone to replace you," said Miss Hood sternly. "This is a gentle piece, not heavy metal."

"Drunk in charge of a tambourine!" muttered Oakley Flangrove.

"Shake it *delicately*, Jackson," said Miss Hood.

Jackson was tired of shaking the tambourine delicately. On the other hand, he certainly didn't want anyone else shaking it in his place. Across

the heads of the recorder players he saw Oakley Flangrove rattle an imaginary tambourine at him, with his little finger sticking out delicately. That was the thing Jackson could not explain to Tracey. Oakley might have big teeth, and a boring, respectable haircut, but Oakley had rhythm, even on a violin.

Outside, a small group of children were waiting to come into the library.

"All right, you can go to recess now," said Miss Hood. "You recorder people had better practice at home tonight."

As he made for the door, Jackson hesitated. An idea had come to him. Almost without thinking about it he made for the library reference shelves and the dictionary . . . not the little one with the big print, but the big dark-blue one. The word *quodlibet* sounded as if it might be a *big* dictionary word, and it wouldn't take long to find. Jackson thought there couldn't be many words beginning with *Q*, which seemed a left-out sort of letter.

All the same, he was surprised at how many there were. Of course a lot of them were weird.

He ran his finger down the page. *Quadrangle, quiff, quoit, quorum* . . . but he had gone too far. Turning back a page or two, moving his finger from word to word, he breathed hard, sticking out his tongue as he always did when concentrating on difficult stuff. Suddenly, there it was: *Quodlibet!* Like magic!

"*Quodlibet,*" he read. "*A scholastic argumentation on a subject chosen at will but almost always theological.*"

The word had a meaning, but the meaning didn't mean anything.

"What are you doing?" asked a voice behind him. Jackson turned and found Oakley Flangrove looking over his shoulder.

"I've found the word," said Jackson, "but the meaning doesn't make sense, man."

"Some words have two meanings," said Oakley, moving off. Jackson looked again and suddenly saw there was indeed another meaning printed under the first one. "*A fanciful harmonic combination of two or more melodies,*" he murmured to himself, because he found it easier to understand written words when he heard them said aloud. "*A medley.*"

Jackson said nothing for a moment. Then he began to look up *bombinate* which turned out to be "hum" or "buzz." The mysterious message seemed to be about singing. But what about *tattoo, tap,* and *tan*? *Tattoo* was easy enough. People had words and pictures tattooed on their skin, and even when their skins were tanned, the tattoos showed. But how did that fit in with a medley, or a humming or buzzing sound? Jackson couldn't work it out.

"Forget it!" he told himself, but he couldn't put it out of his mind. For the rest of the day the rhyme danced through his head.

> *Bam bam bombinate,*
> *Tattoo, tap, and tan.*
> *Quodlibet! Quodlibet!*
> *Ran dan dan!*

And what was the meaning of the egg in an eggcup?

"Jackson, don't click your pen like that," said Miss Hood. Jackson decided to think about the egg in the eggcup later when he could click as much as he wanted to.

CHAPTER 4

The Good Fortunes Gang met on a platform built in a tree. The tree grew on top of a bank next to a track in the forest behind their grandparents' house. On the edge of the forest oaks and maples mixed with the native trees, so that every autumn the forest had a bright fringe of scarlet and yellow. But after the first few steps along the shadowy track, explorers and travelers found themselves in real New Zealand bush, dense, shadowy, closing in overhead, and always green, for these trees did not change color in autumn or lose their leaves in winter.

Tessa was the first to arrive on the platform, even though she had had to leave her bicycle by her grandparents' garden shed. Tracey and Jackson came next. They left their skateboards at the gate, under the mailbox, and raced one another through the garden, in under the trees, up the bank, then up the ladder nailed to the tree trunk. Pete was the fourth to arrive, but they had to wait another ten minutes for Lorelei, because she went to the Catholic school and had farther to come. Besides, she was a careful cyclist.

"You can take off those sunglasses now," Tracey said to Jackson. Suddenly, it was as if everything about him annoyed her. But this was one thing he would not do . . . even for Tracey. He would not take off his sunglasses. He had found them at the beach. Indeed, it sometimes seemed they had *chosen* him. Looking down at just the right moment, he had seen them looking back at him, small, round discs of darkness on the dark sand. When he had put them on for the first time, they had settled on his nose as if they were glad to be there, and sometimes it seemed that the only private space he had in the world was behind his glasses.

"No way, man!" he said to Tracey, pointing to broken shafts of light slicing through the cracks in the rough roof over the platform.

"There's no ultraviolet in here," Tracey said. "You don't look cool. You just look weird."

Jackson simply pushed his glasses farther up his nose.

"Never mind that," Tessa cried. She was setting out the gang's food on the floor between their feet (a big bag of potato chips and some chocolate-chip cookies). "Let's get on with the meeting. There aren't any minutes, and there's no treasurer's report, so I vote we go straight to item one. The prowler!"

"Is there really a prowler?" asked Lorelei.

Tessa cleared her throat.

"Yes," she said, "and I reckon he's planning to burgle our house, now that it's full of jewels and wedding presents."

There was a silence while the gang thought about this.

"That motorcycle?" asked Tracey. "That's nothing much!"

"It's not just the motorcycle," said Tessa. "Two days ago the phone rang, so I picked it up and said 'Hello,' like everyone does—except Jackson. But nothing happened. Nobody said anything. I said 'Tessa here!' about three times, and then it went *click*. Very softly! Just *click*! That was all."

"Wrong number, cucumber!" said Pete. He sometimes talked in rhyme, which proved that he and Jackson were cousins even if they did not look alike.

"Well, that's what I thought, but it's happened more than once," said Tessa. "By now it's happened at least six times. And not just to me. Mom answers the phone, waits, then puts it down. No one there! I reckon someone's checking us out."

"Is that all?" asked Tracey. "So where does the motorcycle come in?"

"I saw it for the first time about two days ago," said Tessa, making her voice deeper and spookier. "In the twilight. It was parked on the opposite side of the road outside that house with the broken gate. Well, I thought someone was visiting the broken-gate people. But when I came out yesterday morning, that very same motorcycle was cruising past our place. It was going very slowly, and the driver was looking straight down our driveway. And that night, when I was drawing the curtains, there he was again—cruising by on the other side of the road. Well, I've watched since then. Didn't see anyone yesterday morning, but last night . . ." She paused dramatically.

". . . there he was!" Jackson finished the sentence for her.

"Right!" said Tessa. "And this morning too. You saw him!"

"So what?" Pete exclaimed. "Perhaps he's just staying with someone in your street."

"No," declared Tessa. "He was quite obviously looking into our place. You couldn't see his face, but you could see which way his helmet was turned."

"Hey, man, suppose this dude is a phantom motorcyclist," said Jackson. "Suppose there was *no face* inside the helmet."

There was a silence while the Good Fortunes Gang thought about this.

"There wouldn't be a phantom motorcyclist going around during the day," said Pete. "If it was midnight . . . well . . . maybe. But not during the day."

"And what about the telephone calls?" said Tessa. "No, it must be prowlers wanting to pinch the wedding presents and Prue's ring."

"They'd have to cut off her hand," said Lorelei in a surprisingly bloodthirsty voice. "You'd find her in the morning lying in bed, with a stump on the end of her arm going drip, drip, drip."

"No," said Tessa crossly. She thought Lorelei was trying to turn her real prowler into a made-up monster. "She doesn't wear that ring all the time. Mom's always after her because she's sort of careless with it. But Mom didn't take any notice when I said we were being spied on by prowlers. She just told me not to be silly."

"Lock your doors and windows," suggested Pete.

"We do already, but we're out a lot," said Tessa. "We have to go and get fitted and pinned up in bridesmaid's clothes. And Prue and Mom go out and listen to music. They're trying to choose a band for the wedding dance. A good prowler could easily break into our house while we were out. We'd come home and the video, and the set of silver knives and forks, and the Portuguese bowl, and the stainless steel saucepans, would all be gone."

"You could borrow the Labradoodle for a watchdog," suggested Tracey.

"*Your* dog? He's too much of a coward," said Tessa scornfully.

"Yes, but he barks loudly," said Tracey. "A prowler wouldn't know he was a coward."

"We have to be prepared for any eventuality,"

Tessa said. She unfolded a map and spread it on the floor of the tree house. "Look! Here's Bright Street."

"Where?" asked Jackson.

"Take off those silly glasses, and you'll be able to see, mong-bat," said Tracey. Jackson was furious. He and Tracey called Leeanne and Katherine "mong-bats," a name they had invented. To have Tracey call him a mong-bat seemed like treachery of the worst kind.

"Hey! don't be so *heavy* with me," he complained. "I haven't done anything."

"My plan," said Tessa, taking no notice of the quarrel, "is that we set up a watch. When we see him again, we'll follow him, and find out where he lives. Then, if the wedding presents do get stolen, we'd be able to point the police in the right direction."

Jackson smiled, imagining a news item on television. "*I wish there were more people like these kids,*" a detective would say. "*They had it all sewn up. We just came in and cleaned up after them.*"

"How can we follow someone on a motorbike?" asked Lorelei.

"Watch the map, will you?" asked Tessa crossly. "He always goes off down Bright Street toward the

playing field. All right! We set a spy up in the Bright Street tree. Perhaps we can borrow Uncle Ivor's cellular phone." She looked hopefully at Lorelei. If Tracey and Jackson's father had had such a thing as a car phone, Tracey would have offered it immediately. Indeed, she often borrowed things without asking first. But Lorelei looked cautious.

"I don't know," she said. "He uses it during the day."

Tessa sighed.

"Well, we'll have a pole with a flag on it. One of us gets onto the roof of the band rotunda over by the playing field and watches the Bright Street tree through Dad's binoculars. You can see it from there. Meanwhile, Tracey and Jackson will be standing by with their skateboards."

"I'd rather . . . well, I'd rather be a bridesmaid than spend all day just waiting for someone to signal," complained Tracey.

Jackson laughed.

"What's funny?" Tracey snapped.

"*You* a bridesmaid?" said Jackson. "That's a laugh."

"Let's give it a go, just once, and see what hap-

pens," bargained Tessa. "Tomorrow evening . . .
about five o'clock."

"All right," said Tracey. "It's something to do, I
suppose."

It was the sort of thing she usually loved. Jackson couldn't think why Tracey was not more
thrilled about it all. Slouching there in the first-
floor boardroom tree house, he felt something rus-
tle in his pocket. It was the clue.

"Owangabangabootabotta!" he muttered to
himself. Not everyone could remember a word like
that, he thought. At last he had a secret life of his
own that nobody else knew about. And there in
the middle of a Good Fortunes Gang meeting he
began to wonder once more just who was trying to
get in touch with him with such dancing words.

CHAPTER 5

"Why don't we *sit* at the table for breakfast?" asked Leeanne plaintively, the following morning. "The Burnses always sit at the table, even for breakfast. And the cups match the saucers too. And they have a butter knife."

"The table is covered with your stuff," her mother answered crossly. "Look . . . Barbie dolls, felt pens, posters of imaginary rock bands, exercise books . . . why don't you tidy your stuff away if you want to have breakfast on the table?"

"Jackson did the drawing," whined Leeanne. "If I have to tidy up, he's got to tidy up too."

A curious piping whistle sounded above the family voices.

"And the sound of the little spotted kiwi announces our seven o'clock news program," said the radio.

"Cornflakes, cornflakes!" sang Leeanne, drumming on the countertop with a spoon. "Who's got the cornflakes?"

She had a good rhythm going, thought Jackson, drumming too. The baby began to fret. Toast leapt up in the toaster as if it were eager to be buttered and eaten. "Toot toot!" yelled Madonna and Jared, the four-year-old twins. They liked to eat their breakfast while riding the tricycle. The Labradoodle, who had heard the toaster, began to bark.

"Toast! Toast!" yelled Jackson, in time to his own rhythm. "Totally excellent! Party on down, man!"

"Jackson, will you stop beating a tattoo with that spoon?" his mother yelled. Jackson stopped.

"Tattoo?" he said. "What do you mean? Tattoo? Tattoos are pictures you have done on you with a needle."

"It's a sort of drumming too," said his mother. "Where's Tracey? I need help. I need someone to hold the baby."

A sort of drumming! *Tattoo* was another sound word, after all.

But then Tracey came into the room, and the word *tattoo* flew out of Jackson's mind immediately. Tracey was wearing a dress.

For as long as Jackson could remember, Tracey had worn shirts, T-shirts, long sloppy sweaters, and blue jeans—always blue jeans. If he ever imagined her as a newborn baby, he saw her quite clearly, bald and howling perhaps, but with tiny blue jeans pulled up over her diaper. Wearing a dress, she resembled a *false* Tracey, a changeling replacing the real one.

Leeanne looked as if she was longing to laugh her head off in secret. The Labradoodle broke the silence with furious barking. But Angel, the baby, beamed, and began bouncing in her mother's arms. She adored Tracey—no matter what she wore.

"What are you mong-bats all staring at?" Tracey asked, looking sternly from one to the other. The Labradoodle's bark changed at the sound of her voice. He began wuffing to himself, as if before he had merely been clearing his throat. Then, realizing that no one was taking any notice of him, he stood on his hind legs and began snuffling along the edge of the table for unguarded toast or cornflakes.

"Hello, kid!" Tracey said to Angel. "I'll hold

you for a bit. Dog! Get down from there!" She took Angel from her mother and pushed the Labradoodle with her foot so that he slid sideways, scrabbling with his paws. He barked again, but Tracey barked back at him so fiercely that he sat down and stared at her pleadingly. She bounced Angel, who screamed with delight.

"You don't look like Trace the Ace in that dress," said Leeanne. "You look like someone else."

"A Barbie doll, I suppose," said Tracey grimly.

"No way!" cried Leeanne, laughing at the thought.

"Why are you wearing that dress?" asked her mother, as if she had only just noticed it. "Is there something on at school I ought to know about?"

"I just wanted to," said Tracey. "I don't always have to wear jeans, you know."

"No, but that dress . . ."

"It's the only dress I've got," said Tracey.

"I know," said Tiffany. "It's such a long time since you wore a dress that I . . . Tracey, it really doesn't go with those running shoes. And . . . oh, dear, it's already far too small for you. Why don't you kids stop growing, just for six months, anyway?"

Jackson's mouth shut and then opened again, like the mouth of a goldfish in an aquarium.

"I know it's a bit short, but it's okay," said Tracey. "It's a hot day. I won't get cold."

"You look weird," said Leeanne.

"You look weird too," said Tracey. "You're the one who looks like a Barbie doll." This was meant as an insult, but Leeanne smiled, pleased with herself.

Tracey moved over to the sink. She lifted the box of cornflakes, then she stopped, the cornflakes box held in midair, and wheeled around to look behind her. Everyone was staring at her, but as she looked back at them, they all quickly pretended to be doing something else. A ripple of movement ran around the entire kitchen. Her mother quickly began fussing over Angel. Leeanne crammed toast into her mouth and crunched loudly, spluttering a few crumbs out at the side. Jackson broke into a dance, moving to music only he could hear. His clue was a sort of song, he was sure of that now. It was about singing and drumming, and it had been sent to him because he was a drummer . . . well, he *would* have been a drummer if he had had a drum.

"Tracey, go and put your jeans on," said Tif-

fany. "I don't want you going to school in a dress that's too small for you."

"I can't be bothered changing now," Tracey answered. "I don't want to get dressed twice in one morning."

An advertisement for garden supplies that no one in the Fortune kitchen was listening to had come to an end.

"And our request of the morning is for Jackson Fortune," said the announcer. Jackson stared around in amazement, but even though his name had been spoken by a radio announcer nobody else in the family had heard it. They were either arguing about Tracey's dress, or enjoying the argument.

"Jackson . . . what we have for you is the Bob Dylan classic 'Mr. Tambourine Man.' And all of us at WBFX hope it gets your day off to a grea-ea-eat beginning."

"Hey! Mr. Tambourine Man, play a song for me," sang Bob Dylan.

"Listen! Listen!" Jackson shouted, but the family argument was too loud. There was shouting backward and forward. He ran to the radio and clapped his ear against it. Though he knew the song quite well, it seemed different this morning, dedicated to him by someone unknown.

Madonna and Jared, who were too young to be tactful, still stood staring at Tracey as if she were something in a zoo.

"What are you kids gawking at?" Tracey yelled at them. There was a slight tearing sound. Stitches had broken loose on Tracey's right shoulder seam.

What's going on? Jackson wondered. *I'm getting messages from outer space, and Tracey's wearing a dress. Perhaps we're being taken over by aliens.*

"All right! Wear it, then!" cried Tiffany despairingly. "You'll be sorry, but that's your lookout. I'm too frazzled to bother anymore."

The song finished. Even though the kitchen was full of people, Jackson's magic moment had come and gone without anyone else noticing.

"And I *am* Mr. Tambourine Man," he said loudly. His words fell into an unexpected silence and everyone looked at him. "Where's my pack?" he asked quickly, though he knew exactly where it was.

"In your room, mong-bat!" said Leeanne. "I saw it lying on the floor. Serve you right if the Labradoodle has torn it to bits."

Jackson suddenly looked anxious. It was true that the Labradoodle thought he was allowed to chew anything he found on the floor.

"But, Mom, all my clothes are too small," argued Tracey in a quieter voice.

"Well, that dress is *much* too small. Why are you suddenly so set on wearing it?"

As Jackson scrambled for his room, he heard Leeanne say in a shrewd voice, "They'll never ever ask you to be a bridesmaid, not in a million years." Jackson came to a stop, shut his eyes, screwed up his face, and waited—as if a blow was going to fall on him rather than on Leeanne. A cry of anguish came from the kitchen.

"Tracey. Say you're sorry! Leeanne, Tracey didn't mean it."

"She did! She did! She *meaned* it because she's *mean*. She's always mean to me. She looks like a terminator," sniveled Leeanne, "and she wants to be a bridesmaid."

"I do not!" yelled Tracey. "I look—I look like everyone else. And I don't want to be a bridesmaid, anyway."

Jackson ran off to his own dark corner with a strong feeling that he wanted to hide in his bunk and not come out again until Tracey had taken the dress off and put on her blue jeans, her true jeans, her true skin.

He grabbed up his pack. A big square blue envelope slid off it and lay on the floor. *Owangaban-gabootabotta!* he read in colored letters. Another clue, but this time it had appeared in his own house, in his very own room, on his very own pack. He picked it up and stared around as if the walls might whisper, or a thin, echoing voice might come out of the light-shade overhead. The window was shut. There was nowhere to hide.

As Jackson tore the envelope open he was impressed to find his fingers trembling a little. That proved how exciting life had become. At first he had been sorry that the rest of his family had been too noisy to hear his name come over the radio, but now he was glad. The mystery was his and his alone.

> *What you're needing is a lotta*
> *Whangabangabootabotta.*
> *Come and join a lotta friends.*
> *Burn the candle at both ends.*
> *One points up and five points down.*
> *Three's the hippest house in town.*
> *Can you solve this riddle diddle?*
> *Find the three that's in the middle?*
> *But your sister is a blister.*
> *Bootabotta and resist her.*

CHAPTER 6

"Okay, let's rock and roll!" yelled Jackson from the porch. But Tracey had set out without him. She was already halfway to the Main Road corner. Behind, he could hear Leeanne saying, "I'll be at Katherine's place, or Desdemona's, or else at Annabel's."

"Who's Annabel?" their mother asked.

"You know Annabel! She lives at the other end of Katherine's street."

Jackson barely heard them. He was too busy staring after Tracey. He could not believe it. She did not have her skateboard with her. She was actually walking. Jackson shot off after her.

"What's the story, morning glory?" he cried, coming up behind her.

"I'm bored with skateboarding," said Tracey. "You don't have to wait for me."

Jackson wondered if she could read his mind and make out the riddle bobbing about there. It seemed to be a sort of invitation . . . but whoever it was who was inviting him, clearly did not want Tracey too. Someone wanted him to work out the clue, then run off, leaving Tracey on her own. Jackson would not do this. It would be mean to desert her.

"Hey," said Jackson. "You're walking! Okay, I'll walk too. We're a team, man." Tracey had always told him they were a team.

Now she wheeled on him.

"Stop calling me 'man'!" she hissed. Just for a moment she looked at him with cold, snakelike eyes.

"Hey, cool it!" cried Jackson hastily. Tracey spun around and stalked off ahead of him. Jackson straightened his sunglasses and hurried after her, glad to hide his own eyes behind those blank dark shades.

Tracey walked with stiff, small footsteps, though she managed to go quite fast, almost as if she was trying to leave him behind. Jackson glided slowly after her, feeling like the Labradoodle forced to go for a walk with someone who did not want to take him. Here was a chance to glide off with no one ahead of him, and yet something was wrong. He did not feel free to go.

As they approached the Bright Street tree, they saw Tessa was waiting for the second day running. She looked at Tracey but did not recognize her for a moment. Then her eyes and her mouth grew round in her already round face. Tessa became one big "oh!" of surprise.

"You're wearing a *dress!*" she cried.

Tracey sighed impatiently. "So what?" she asked. "Other people wear dresses."

"Yes, but not *you!*" said Tessa.

"No way, man," said Jackson. Tracey turned. As she turned, Jackson distinctly heard her dress tear. Tracey clapped her hand to her waist as if she had been stabbed in her side. She looked frightened for the fraction of a second, then furious.

"Get out!" she yelled at him. "Don't *follow* me all the time. Everywhere I go, I have to have you hanging around me, putting your oar into everything. Everyone must think I *have* to have you with me all the time."

Jackson jumped off his skateboard, flipped it up, tried to catch it in midair, and missed. It fell at his feet. Amazed by this angry stranger, he barely noticed it.

"Go some *other* way to school," ordered Tracey. "I don't want you listening in on everything I say."

Tessa stared from Tracey to Jackson in consternation.

"What's wrong?" she asked.

"Nothing," said Tracey. "I just want . . . I don't know . . . I want some other sort of life for a bit. Come on! Don't take any notice of *him*."

She stalked off, still holding one hand at her waist, and after a minute Tessa followed her. Jackson gathered up his skateboard and stood in the middle of the sidewalk behind them, watching them go. Tessa looked back once, opening her mouth as if she might call out a kind word, but Tracey did not turn. In the blue dress that was certainly much too small for her, she moved away from him—still a sister, yet suddenly a stranger—leaving him stranded on the sidewalk.

Only yesterday, Jackson had been longing to glide along sidewalks without always having Tracey in front of him. Now, for the first time he could really remember, he felt alone in the world.

But your sister is a blister, the riddle had said.

Other words formed in Jackson's mind.

The day is rancid, rough, and rotten.
Sister gone, but not forgotten.

He had wanted to be on his own, but he certainly hadn't wanted Tracey to turn on him like that, especially when he didn't know why. It was a riddle every bit as baffling as the one in his pocket, and for the moment he couldn't think of an answer to either of them.

CHAPTER
7

When the bell for going home rang, Jackson half expected, in spite of everything, to find Tracey waiting for him. However, there was no sign of her. Kids streamed by him, all with somewhere to go; but Jackson waited.

After a while he felt silly just standing in the school yard, staring at the sky. He didn't quite want to go home, and he didn't have anywhere else to go. Pushing himself off on his faithful skateboard, he wondered if quarreling with Tracey meant that he had stopped being a member of the Good Fortunes Gang. After all, he was the youngest, and he had always had the feeling that the other cousins only put up with him for Tracey's sake. If he turned up at the platform in the tree, might they pull up the rope ladder and send him away?

Jackson left school by a gate that he and Tracey never used, skirted a bus waiting to collect children who lived in the country, and set off. Leaving by this new gate made him feel suddenly free. Forget Tracey! He, Excellent Jack, had a mystery that was all his own, and for once he actually had time to think about it.

Jackson was planning to solve the clue he had found that morning. How exactly had it turned up beside his bed? Had it fallen *out* of his backpack, or had it been lying on top of it? Jackson half hoped it had been sneaked into his backpack at school the day before. It was spooky to think of some unknown person standing beside his bed, clue in hand, watching him while he slept.

Once the school was out of sight, Jackson stopped and sat down by the roadside. He arranged his skateboard neatly beside him, scrummaged in his backpack for the envelope, and slid the clue out. He didn't bother with yesterday's clue. He knew that one by heart now. Both clues had the same egg-in-an-eggcup signature. What did the drawing of an egg suggest? His father sometimes said of someone, "That chap's a bad egg." Jackson considered this but decided the egg in the drawing wasn't a bad egg. The eggcup was crosshatched with brown and green lines, while the base was green. The egg itself was carefully drawn. If ever he had seen a *good* egg, this was it. Could the signature be a way of *egging him on?* Or did it mean that the writer of the clue was an *egghead?* Or simply that the writer was someone very like Jackson himself . . . *as like as two eggs.* But it couldn't be that, he realized. There was only one egg at the bottom of the clue.

The first clue had been about rhythm. He was sure of that. *"Bam bam bominate,"* he said to himself. *Tan* meant to beat something, as well as meaning to sun yourself until you went brown. *Tattoo,* he now knew, could mean a signal on a drum.

What about the song on the radio that morning . . . "Mr. Tambourine Man"? Another musical clue. And then, almost immediately after the song was over, the clue he was holding in his hand had ordered him to shake off Tracey . . . *Bootabotta,* the line advised him, *and resist her.* Well, he hadn't exactly booted her botta, and he hadn't exactly resisted her, but here he was, on his own, thinking about the candle burning at both ends, as well as the numbers.

Jackson knew clues were tricky things. You thought they meant one thing, and then they turned out to mean something quite different. *Burn the candle at both ends.* When his father got up early and worked late, Jackson's mother would say, "That's just like your dad. All Fortunes burn the candle at both ends." But this didn't seem to mean anything useful, and it certainly did not fit in with any of the *drumming* clues. Jackson looked up into the sky, but there was no inspiration in the clouds that were lolloping slowly across the blue.

Jackson's face grew dreamy, his eyes almost but not quite shut, as he beat out an imaginary drumroll on the air. However, they were open enough to notice the motorcyclist in a red helmet who suddenly appeared from between trees farther down the road, and shot past him.

There were many red motorcycle helmets in Fairfield, but not very many with golden stars. He recognized this one immediately. At once a picture formed in his mind of a typical meeting in the Good Fortunes Gang tree. He would be there, of course, Excellent Jack, leaning against his favorite branch, looking totally cool and in control, letting the older kids talk and argue themselves into silence. Then his voice would make itself heard, saying casually, "Oh, by the way, I know where that motorcyclist goes when he's not hanging around outside Tessa's gate." The others would turn to him with expressions of amazement and admiration. No one would look more admiring than Tracey.

Unmistakable though he had been, the motorcyclist had come and gone in a few seconds, and Jackson could not possibly have followed him. What he could do, though, was to find out where the motorcyclist might have come from. Leaping to his feet, and onto his skateboard, Jackson sailed off, urgently glancing up and down the road. No cars! No bikes! The way was clear. "Concentrate!" Jackson told himself. "Don't fall!" Then, leaving the sidewalk, he triumphantly jumped the gutter and shot up and over the small rise of the road almost as skillfully as Tracey herself might have done. Wobbling for a moment, he recovered, ran up where someone had cemented the entryway to their garage, then shot down the opposite sidewalk, toward the trees and bushes from which the motorcyclist had seemed to emerge so magically. *Abracadabra!* thought Jackson. *Now you see him, now you don't.*

There was a street tucked in among the trees—

a short, narrow street, sloping sharply to join the main road. Jackson glimpsed cars going by. Had the motorcyclist used this steep street as a short-cut, or had he actually come out of one or another of the six gateways, three on either side, that opened onto it?

The houses in this road were large and rambling, with big gardens full of trees, so that from where he stood, it looked as if they had been built in a forest. Even though Jackson was concentrating on the gateways and the vanished motorcyclist, he couldn't help listening to music coming from somewhere. Sunlight, falling through the leaves, made the steep slope in front of him dappled and mysterious. Then, as if he had had a vision, Jackson saw a big shining 5 on the gatepost on the opposite corner, and the clue suddenly bobbed to the surface of his thoughts again. Why? *One points up and five points down* . . . Jackson glanced up at the street sign. It seemed, then, that a great mixture of things rushed together in his head, whirled around there, and made a marvelous pattern. CANDLE LANE, the street sign said. Candle Lane! As he stared at the word, *candle* looking so ordinary yet so amazing, he realized something else. That house on the corner was where Lee-anne's friend, Katherine Burns, lived.

Katherine Burns! What was a collector of Barbie dolls doing dancing in the head of a cool drummer? Yet there she was, dancing and talking. Jackson found himself remembering Leeanne's voice almost as if she were beside him now, speaking in his ear. "I'll be at Katherine's place, or Desdemona's, or else at Annabel's."

"Who's Annabel?" his mother had asked.

"You know Annabel. She lives at the other end of Katherine's street."

Jackson did not know whether or not his mother knew Annabel, but he suddenly realized that *he* did. She was Katherine's cousin, Annabel Burns, another member of the Barbie-Doll Club. Katherine Burns at one end of Candle Lane, Annabel Burns at the other! Burns at both ends! Jackson could hardly believe it. Was he solving the clue, or was this all a mistake . . . a fantastic accident? Could something that fitted so neatly possibly be wrong? Jackson pulled faces at the air. Katherine Burns! Annabel Burns! Leeanne! Were all these clues nothing but a Barbie-Doll Club trick? Could little kids . . . mere eight-year-olds . . . invent clues that had been too difficult (*al-*

most too difficult) for Excellent-Jack-sharp-as-a-tack to solve? "Ha! Ha!" Jackson said aloud, sneering at the thought. Through the tops of trees the dormer windows of the Burnses' house stared back at him, like eyes hooded by eyelids. Jackson took a step toward it, and stopped. After all, this was not the place the clue was directing him to find.

One points up and five points down! Jackson looked down Candle Lane counting the gates. If No. 5, Katherine's house, was at the top of the lane, No. 1, Annabel's house, would be at the bottom, and that meant No. 3, the hottest house in town, must be the one between them.

Jackson felt dizzy with the way things were working out. No. 3 was where the music was coming from, and now that he was listening with real attention, he could hear that it wasn't a tape or a record. Real people were singing and playing real guitars in a garden so full of trees, he could barely make out the house beyond. Not only that, he could easily make out the words of the song because he knew them already.

> *Bam bam bombinate*
> *Tattoo, tap, and tan.*

Quodlibet! Quodlibet!
Ran dan dan!

And then the chorus, *Owangabangabootabotta!*
Wangabangabootabotta! Wangabangabootabotta! Bot-
tabootaBANG!

Candle Lane was too steep for a skateboard.
Jackson tucked his skateboard under one arm and
strode down Candle Lane. He went quite confi-
dently in at the gate and under the green trees,
knowing he had been invited. There in front of
him was a house, and on the wide veranda was a
band made up of two boys and a girl. The girl and
one of the boys he vaguely knew, but the second
boy was Oakley Flangrove, playing not a violin but
a guitar. As for the girl, she sat behind something
that thrilled Jackson to the core . . . a complete
set of drums. Fixing his eyes on those drums, he
moved forward like a boy under a spell. Oakley saw
him first.

"Hey! Mr. Tambourine Man!" he shouted. "He
worked it out," he added over his shoulder to the
other two as if he didn't quite believe it.

"You invited me, man!" Jackson called back.
"It would have been rude not to turn up."

CHAPTER 8

At the very moment that Jackson was being welcomed by Oakley Flangrove, his cousins, Tessa and Lorelei, were being pinned into floating panels of pink organza, his other cousin, Pete, was biking toward a small shopping center to pick up a bag of onions that his mother had paid for but had left on the floor in the grocer's, and his sister, Tracey, was standing outside a hair salon staring through the door with horror. The thing that horrified her was her own reflection, which, for the first time that day, she could clearly see.

During the day Tracey's dress had split in two directions—downward under the arms, and sideways across one shoulder. The gathers at the waist had stretched and torn free from the top. Worry about the dress stopped her worrying too much about Jackson. She knew she had been mean to him, but he had driven her mad, constantly telling people that she did not want to be a bridesmaid just at the time she was trying so hard to show them, without having to *tell* them, that she did. Tracey certainly did not want Jackson standing around when she actually asked her aunt (or her cousin Prue) if she, Trace the Ace, could be a bridesmaid at Prue's wedding. She had worn the dress that morning so that they would see that she *could* wear a dress if she wanted to. Now the treacherous dress was falling to pieces.

Tracey had borrowed the stapler from the teacher's desk and stapled her skirt back onto the top. But ten minutes later she sneezed and the dress burst open once more. A torn edge she could not see tapped like a ghost at her shoulder.

For the first time in her life Tracey wished she were the sort of girl who carried pins around with her. After lunch she tried holding herself together with paper clips, but they kept sliding off and losing themselves. And through this crotchety anxious school day, in between trying to hold her dress together, she thought uneasily about the way she had walked away from her faithful follower,

Jackson, just because he sneered at bridesmaids—something she had often done herself. By the time school ended, she had decided to forgive him and allow him to follow her as usual. But after school she was delayed, having to fasten herself together with a completely new set of paper clips. When at last she went out into the playground, walking as delicately as she could, Jackson was not there.

Tracey couldn't believe it. Jackson had actually gone off on his own. A strange, deserted feeling swept over her. How can you feel like a leader if there is nobody waiting to be led? All she could do was to set off for Tessa's house just as she had been planning to do since she woke up that morning.

The closer she came to Bright Street, the more uneasy she grew. Would the paper clips hold? Would anyone else notice her dress was just slightly on the ragged side? Going past the open door of the Top Story Hair Salon, she glanced in at the door. Suddenly she saw herself reflected in a tall mirror beside the cash register and stopped aghast. Who was that lanky girl wearing a blue dress that made her legs look even longer, and her scratched knees even more knobbly? Who was that girl with grubby running shoes as big as battleships? *That can't be me*, thought Tracey. But it was.

Vital paper clips had already fallen away, and the soft blue material strained across her chest and shoulders, ready to tear again at any moment.

At home it had seemed that, if she breathed carefully and moved gently, the dress would hold together and nobody would notice it was too small. All day Tracey had *suffered* in order to look unexpectedly beautiful, but the suffering had been for nothing. No one would ever look at her and say "Good heavens! Is that Tracey Fortune? What a wonderful bridesmaid *she* would make!"

Tracey stared at her reflection. Then she shrugged. Somewhere the dress tore a little more, but she was past caring.

"I'm sick of this," she said to herself. "They'll never ask me. Okay, I'll ask them. And I'll do it now."

She set off for Tessa's house, practicing arguments as to why she should be a bridesmaid by muttering them softly to herself to see how they sounded.

"There ought to be a bridesmaid from every family. I know you think I'm not a *bridesmaid* sort of girl, but I don't mind being a bridesmaid, just once. I'll really try. I know I can do it. After that

I'll go back to being a skateboarder and never wear a dress again."

Tracey was so involved in her own plans, she did not see her cousin, Pete, biking past. He was chanting softly under his breath. "My mother's feet are sore with bunions, so *I* must go and get the onions." His mother hadn't quite said that, but there aren't many words that rhyme with *onions* and Pete always enjoyed a rhyme or two. He pressed his own feet down on the pedals in time to his words.

As Tracey came down the drive on one side of Tessa's house she saw the garage was open and empty. The only car in the yard was Prue's old Volkswagen. Tracey came to a stop. Now was the time to act . . . now, before Aunt Marama and Tessa arrived home. Yet Tracey felt her courage draining away.

Someone spoke her name. It was the bride-to-be, Cousin Prue, looking out of an open window. She was wearing one of the strange hats she made herself, and she was studying Tracey from under the gold tassels that hung around the brim. She looked as if she might burst into laughter at any moment, even though she knew she shouldn't.

"Mom's taken Tessa and Lorelei into town,"

said Prue. "They'll be back soon. Would you like to have some ice cream while you wait?"

Tracey took a deep breath. "I don't want ice cream," she said. "What I want is to be a bridesmaid at your wedding, like Tessa and Lorelei."

Prue's expression changed, but she didn't seem taken aback or dismayed. She replied without hesitation, saying the most beautiful words in the world.

"Why not?" she said. "I've always wanted three bridesmaids. Three's a lucky number. Come on in, and bring your dress with you . . . if you can. We'll talk it over."

Meanwhile, at the dressmaker's, things were not going so smoothly for Tessa.

"Ow!" her cousin Tessa was crying rebelliously. She had turned to argue with her mother, clapping her hands to her hips as she did so, and a pin had run into her finger.

"Don't bleed on that organdy," her mother was shouting. "Hold your hand out over the floor! Why can't you stand still like Lorelei does?"

"Because I'm starving," cried Tessa. "I haven't had a single thing to eat since lunch."

"Funny," said the dressmaker, "you actually seem a little bit fatter than you did at the last fitting."

And on the north side of Fairfield, at No. 3 Candle Lane, Jackson was drumming wildly. Rhythm ran like electricity down his arms. He felt completely powerful at last.

Owangabangabootabotta!

He sang with the other members of the band, and ended by crashing the drumsticks down, laughing as he did so. He hadn't had so much fun for a long time. Great words! Great song!

"Did you really solve the clue?" asked the boy with the saxophone. His name was Kester. He was Oakley's big brother. "I didn't think anyone would actually solve it."

Jackson knew it was only an accident that had put him in the right place at the right time.

"It was absolutely, utterly easy," said the girl, Oakley's even bigger sister, Portia. Tracey was right, thought Jackson. The Flangroves were a weird family with weird names, but it didn't matter —not when they owned a complete set of drums.

"Once you saw the signature you must have known where to come," said Portia.

"Yeah, man!" Jackson cried, secretly wondering what possible sort of signature the egg in the eggcup had been.

"I mean, if you get a mysterious clue signed with an acorn, the thickest idiot would immediately think of Oakley," Portia cried.

Not an egg in an eggcup! An acorn! Oakley Flangrove, who lived among oak trees, had signed himself with an acorn. Jackson smiled just as if he had known all along.

"I worked out the bit about the candle burning at both ends, because I knew where Katherine Burns lived," he boasted, which was almost true. But would he have solved the clue if the motorcyclist in the red helmet hadn't suddenly popped out of Candle Lane? And where exactly had the motorcyclist come from? Jackson didn't have time to think about this because Kester was explaining something.

"We're starting a band," said Kester. "*I* want to call it the Scumbags."

"Kester, you are not to give your band a revolting name like that," said Mrs. Flangrove, who happened to be walking across the veranda at that moment. As she vanished through the front door, Jackson heard from somewhere in the middle of the house the sound of a lot of small girls all giggling at once, and the sound of someone practicing the piano. Oakley's house was filled with people and music. Jackson had the feeling that if ten unexpected visitors came trooping up the path, Mrs. Flangrove would simply smile and say "Go on in! You know where the cookies are."

"We'll have to give our band some sissy name to go on with," Oakley muttered to Jackson, "until we're making money. The thing is, we need a drummer, because Portia wants to play the second guitar."

"I wanted a girl drummer," said Portia, "but then Oakley said you were really good. He said you got told off for drumming at school even though you didn't have any drums."

"Of course we had to get you away from Trace the Ace," Oakley explained. "I didn't think you'd ever really escape. How did you do it?" Jackson opened his mouth, but Oakley didn't really want an explanation. "The next thing we do is to set up a gig or two," he said grandly.

"What's a gig?" asked Jackson.

"A gig's *work* . . . a performance," said

Kester. "We need somewhere to play so people can hear us."

Jackson's heart leapt. He might not have guessed the acorn clue, and he might have stumbled accidentally into solving the others, but he, Jackson, knew of a possible gig. Only yesterday he had heard Tessa say that her mother and Prue were wanting to choose a band for the wedding dance. He smiled, opened his mouth, then shut it again, remembering something. The Flangroves were related to Prue's first rascally, runaway husband. She might not want a band with two Flangroves in it. Still, it was worth a try, thought Jackson.

"Let's run through it all from the top," Kester was saying.

"Hang on!" Jackson cried. "I have to call someone at home about something. Where's the phone?"

"Down the hall and in the kitchen," said Portia. "Just go straight down the hall."

Jackson set off, glad that the Oakleys' house was the sort of house where a visitor could easily look for the phone himself. Until he had talked to Prue, he wanted his phone call to be a secret from the rest of the band.

CHAPTER 9

As Marama Fortune drove Tessa and Lorelei back from Mrs. Harper's, the dressmaker, Tessa suddenly saw Pete standing outside the ice-cream shop, looking like someone who was planning to buy something delicious. She was so hungry, her stomach felt as if it were shrinking down to the size of a walnut.

"Stop! Stop!" she called. "There's Pete. We'll walk home with him."

"Oh, all right! I have to stop anyway," said her mother, pulling into a parking space. "We need extra milk."

"Ice creams?" Tessa asked eagerly, half holding out her hand.

"No!" said her mother. "You're too fat as it is.

Mrs. Harper says you've put on weight since last week."

"She just said that because she'd pinned me up wrongly," whined Tessa. "This wedding's killing me." But her mother was unyielding.

Lorelei and Tessa scrambled out of the car and pelted down the sidewalk.

"Pete might have some money," groaned Tessa. "People say I think about money too much, but you absolutely *need* it, or you starve."

"Hi!" they shouted in Pete's ear, and he spun around, twitching with fright.

"Have you got any money on you?" asked Tessa. "I've got ten cents but it's not enough for ice cream, and I'm starving!"

Pete shook his head. His fright, though, seemed to be lasting longer than was strictly necessary. At any rate he was staring past them, round eyed, as if had seen something astonishing on the other side of the road.

"Well, never mind!" said Tessa. "Let's whiz home, steal a supply of cookies, because we'll need sugar for energy, and then we'll set up our surveillance system in case the motorcyclist comes spying again tonight."

Pete spoke in an odd voice.

"There he is now. Right behind you!"

"What?" exclaimed Tessa and Lorelei, both turning.

On the other side of the road was a garage and car repair shop with a yard of wrecked cars between them. Pete was right. The motorcyclist with the red helmet was just turning in at the garage, and a man in overalls, wiping grease off his hands with a blue cloth, was coming to meet him, grinning as if he was greeting a friend. The helmeted man leapt off his motorcycle. They clapped each other on the shoulder, then sat down on the low brick wall that stood between the yard and the sidewalk and began gossiping.

"What a chance!" hissed Tessa. "Okay, everyone . . . split up so we don't look like a gang, and walk over to that side of the road. Just act casual."

"I'm casual enough already," said Lorelei, looking down at herself. "What do we do when we get there?"

"Listen in," suggested Pete. "See if he's saying anything about robbing Tessa's house." Then he laughed.

"It's not a joke!" said Tessa crossly. "I'm totally sure there's something funny going on, and I want

73

to know what it is. Don't come if you don't want to."

She herself set off across the road, acting casual. For Tessa this meant whistling while looking around in all directions, and then pretending to wave to nonexistent friends in the distance.

"I'm supposed to take these onions home," said Pete uncertainly.

"Oh, come on," said Lorelei. "It's so exciting! He'll probably take off in a minute, and then everything will be boring again and you can take the onions home. Look at Tessa! I'm going to act casual too."

Tessa was prancing along toward the two men on the sunny brick wall. She had already walked past them once. Now, she turned and came back again, slightly red in the face from whistling casually. "Hi!" she called, smiling and waving at an imaginary friend far down Main Road.

"I'm not going to whistle," said Lorelei, turning back to confide in Pete. "Two people whistling might make it look suspicious. I'm just going to skip along." Lorelei's skipping was almost as hopeless as Tessa's whistling. Pete decided against either skipping or whistling. He thought it would be better to slouch past, swinging the bag of onions.

The two men barely glanced at all the casual skipping, whistling, slouching, and onion swinging going on behind them. They got to their feet, walked over to the motorcycle, and looked at it together. The red helmet seemed to be boasting about it, while the other man nodded sympathetically. At last the red-helmeted man mounted his motorcycle again. Pete waited for the engine to leap to life, carrying him out of their lives once more. But the engine failed to start.

"Oh, no!" the man cried in irritation. They all heard him this time. As he sat astride his motorbike they could see that under his jacket he was wearing an old blue T-shirt with a golden sun painted on it.

"What's up?" said the other.

"I've lost my key!" Pete heard the man in the red helmet say. "I can't have." He began going through his pockets. "I've just been standing here yakking away. I haven't been anywhere else." He moved back to the wall and looked on it and then on either side of it, but he couldn't find it.

"Luckily I've got a spare," Pete heard the red helmet say. "I'll walk back home and get it. It's just around the corner."

"Well, your bike'll be safe here," said the other man. "No worries!"

The motorcyclist didn't remove his helmet, but walked off, passing within an arm's length of Tessa. Out in the street, without his motorcycle, he looked rather like a man from outer space exploring an alien planet.

Tessa stared after him with an odd expression.

"Did you see what he was wearing under his jacket? That painted T-shirt?" she asked.

"Forget his T-shirt! What do we do now?" muttered Pete, watching the red helmet striding down the road. Tessa recovered first.

"Follow him!" she exclaimed. "He can't go whizzing away from us this time."

"Let him get a little start, though, so he won't notice we're trailing him," Pete added quickly. Lorelei said nothing. She, too, had a peculiar expression on her face. She looked mischievous, but she looked frightened too. Tessa stared at her.

"What's wrong?" she asked. "Do you have to get home early?"

"I've done something terrible," said Lorelei. Her voice came out in a strange, wailing whisper. Then she dangled a key in front of their astonished eyes. "He left it on the wall there and I just skipped by, acting casual, and picked it up. I've stolen his key. Now what'll I do?"

Pete and Tessa were too astounded to say a word.

"My hand just sneaked out and snatched it up," Lorelei said apologetically. "And then, when I had it, I couldn't put it down again."

The motorcyclist was by now a long way away. As he took off his helmet at last, the cousins could see he had black curls. Something about the back of his head suggested that if they could see his face they would find he was very handsome.

"Don't worry . . . we'll get the key back to him," said Tessa. "But just for now let's follow him and see where he goes."

"Like real detectives," said Pete.

"Yes," said Tessa. "But if he turns around we mustn't look as if we're following him. Just act casual."

CHAPTER
10

At the very moment when other members of the Good Fortunes Gang were beginning to track the motorcyclist, Jackson was taking the Flangroves' kitchen telephone from the top of the refrigerator. He had had to search quite hard for it, but when he found it he wondered why he hadn't seen it at once. Perhaps it was because it didn't look like the sort of phone he was used to. It was shaped like Mickey Mouse, and was standing among a lot of other stuff in a kitchen that was just as untidy as the kitchen at home. However, it was a much bigger kitchen so that the mess was spread out more.

Jackson dialed Uncle Findlay's home number and listened impatiently to the urgent ring at the other end of the line. His luck was in. Prue herself answered the call.

"Excellent-Jack-sharp-as-a-tack," Jackson announced triumphantly.

"Well, how are you, Excellent Jack?" asked Prue. "What can I do for you?"

("Is that Jackson?" demanded a voice in the background.)

"Do you need a band to play at your wedding?" Jackson asked, getting right down to it.

"Of course I do," said Prue. "No band, no dancing! And everyone wants to dance at a wedding."

"But have you *chosen* a band?" Jackson asked breathlessly.

"No, not yet," said Prue. "My mom's doing the choosing for this wedding. Sometimes I think she's really the one who chose Chris to be bridegroom. Mind you, I've just chosen an extra bridesmaid, so that's something, isn't it?"

"Choose a band," said Jackson, interrupting her. He didn't want to hear the word *bridesmaid* ever again. "I know this really *wicked* band! It hasn't got a name yet. At least someone wants to call it the Scumbags, but he's not allowed to."

"I'm glad of that," said Prue. "I don't think

Scumbags quite gets the wedding atmosphere, do you?"

"I'm the drummer," Jackson explained. "We've been practicing, and we are totally *e-e-excellent*."

"Hang on a moment," said Prue. "Let me get this straight. You are the drummer in a band, and you think your band might add a bit of class to my wedding."

"Right on!" said Jackson, pleased that she understood so well. The background voice said something. Jackson could not make out what it was, but it sounded critical.

"I'd have to *hear* the band first," said Prue. "How about coming around and giving me an audition? Tracey and I would both enjoy that."

"Is *Tracey* there?" Jackson cried. His alarm was so great, it was like getting an electric shock. Tracey mustn't see him playing in a band with the Flangroves . . . not yet, not while they were still practicing.

"The drums are hard to move," he said. "Could you come around and listen to us here?"

Rather to his surprise Prue seemed to think about this.

"Why not!" she said. "I'll have to drive Tracey home anyway. I don't want her clothes dropping off in public. Actually I think she'd better borrow Tessa's tracksuit."

"What?" cried Jackson, confused.

"I see you aren't up with the latest developments," Prue said. "Never mind, Excellent Jack. Where are you?"

"I'm at Oakley Flangrove's," said Jackson. Prue laughed again.

"The Flangroves'!" she said. "Is this a Flangrove band? Nice try, Jackson, but you'd better ask them if they want to play at my wedding before we make any definite arrangements."

As Jackson hung up, one of the kitchen doors burst open, and he heard squeaky voices he knew all too well. Four girls began trooping past him. Katherine Burns, Annabel Burns, Desdemona Flangrove, and Leeanne Fortune were all carrying Barbie dolls, and talking to one another in Barbie-doll voices. The Barbie-Doll Club was obviously having a meeting at the Flangroves'.

Leeanne did not notice Jackson immediately.

"I'm getting sick of my boyfriend, Ken," she said, waving her Barbie in front of her as if the doll were talking. "I want a boyfriend who makes good jokes."

"Barbie *has* to have Ken for a boyfriend," said Annabel Burns in an ordinary voice.

"No, she doesn't," said Leeanne. "My Barbie's going to have a clown for a boyfriend." And then she saw Jackson.

"Are *you* the spy who put that clue in my room?" Jackson cried.

Leeanne hesitated, trying to work out if he was angry or pleased about it.

"Was it spooky finding it there first thing in the morning?" asked Desdemona Flangrove, looking pleased. "Did you solve the clue?"

"He must have, because here he is," said Leeanne proudly.

Jackson smiled in a superior way, trying to suggest that such clues were nothing to a brain like his.

"Oakley wanted you to play the drums, but Kester and Portia didn't want you because you're a Fortune," Desdemona said. "*And* you're a cousin of Prue Kennedy's."

It was strange hearing Prue called Prue Kennedy. In the family she was still referred to as Prue Fortune.

"So what?" asked Jackson. "Our band is probably going to play at her wedding."

The small girls stared at him.

"They can't," said Desdemona. "She's already married to Sy."

"She's divorced from him," said Jackson. "She's allowed to get married again. And anyway, he ran off to Australia, and she's never heard from him again. *And* she's had to look after Janey all by herself."

"It was *her* fault," said Desdemona. "They were married for ten months and then *she* was the one who ran away . . . ran home to Mommy just because the kitchen flooded and they had a fight. And she wouldn't let Sy see Janey."

"No way, man," said Jackson. "Everyone knows he ran off to Australia first."

"He came over from Melbourne when he heard she was engaged again," cried Desdemona. "He's tried to talk to her, but she won't even answer the phone."

"Who won't answer the phone?" asked a new voice. A young man walked into the kitchen. He had black hair and eyebrows that met over his nose. The sleeves of his blue T-shirt were pushed up, revealing arms tattooed with dragons.

"Nothing!" said Desdemona quickly. "We were just making up a Barbie story. Come on, you kids."

The Barbie-Doll Club edged out of the kitchen, leaving Jackson alone with the young man. He sighed deeply and put his red motorcycle helmet on the table.

"I could murder a can of Coke," he said, moving toward the fridge. Then he added over his shoulder, "Which one are you?"

"I'm the drummer," Jackson said proudly.

"I meant which Fortune? You Fortunes . . . you're everywhere—like parking meters. Three of you were dancing around me down by the shops, and not only that, they've followed me all the way home."

Jackson stared at him. He was sharing the same room as the motorcyclist, and it seemed that the motorcyclist was Prue's runaway first husband, Sy Kennedy. And Sy was obviously at home here. Jackson, fascinated, watched him choosing a can of Coke from inside the fridge door.

"So, Prue's marrying Chris Moody?" he said, with his back to Jackson.

Jackson couldn't help boasting a little about an important almost-relative. Besides, he was anxious to show Sy Kennedy that he hadn't been missed.

"She's having a wedding with bridesmaids, and then a dance afterward," he said.

"Change from the first time she was married," Sy remarked. "Oh, well," he added, strolling toward the door, "at least she'll have a nice warm house. You're that much closer to the sun up there on the hill. She'll like that. She always loved sunshine. Good luck to her." And he was gone.

Jackson hesitated. After a moment of deep thinking he rang Prue's number again.

But it was not Prue who answered the phone. This time it was Tracey.

"Is Prue there?" he asked, trying to disguise his voice.

"Hey, Jackson!" Tracey cried. She sounded completely happy. "Janey woke up, and Prue's gone to fuss over her. Jackson, guess what? I'm going to be a bridesmaid at Prue's wedding."

Jackson was so astounded, he forgot what he had been calling about.

"I didn't know you wanted to be a bridesmaid," he cried.

"Well, I did," said Tracey. "I don't have to tell you everything in my life."

"Well, *I'm* a member of a band," Jackson boasted quickly.

"It's not that I'm so crazy about actually *being* a bridesmaid," Tracey explained, not really listening to Jackson. "But I hate it when people don't ask me first."

"I'm the drummer," Jackson cried. "They've got a whole set of drums, and I'm in total control. And Prue says we might be able to play at her wedding."

And then he remembered Sy Kennedy once more.

"Sorry I was a bit crabby this morning," Tracey was saying. "Hey, come around to the Bright Street corner. Tessa'll be home soon, and we'd better have a go at catching up with that motorcyclist, just to get her off our backs."

"No," said Jackson. "Listen! The motorcyclist is here. In this house."

"What house! Where are you?"

Tracey still sounded so happy, Jackson felt he could safely tell her the truth.

"At the Flangroves'!" he confessed. The phone immediately hissed like a serpent. It seemed to quiver in his hand.

"The Flangroves'!" shouted Tracey. "Jackson, you come home at once. Right this minute!"

"No," said Jackson boldly. "I'm going to practice with the band."

"That motorcyclist must be a Flangrove *spy*," cried Tracey.

"No, he isn't," Jackson said. "I know who he is. He's Prue's first husband, Sy Kennedy. I was just calling up to warn her."

The phone went quiet. Jackson thought he must have infuriated Tracey into silence.

"Are you still there?" he asked.

"What's he here for?" asked Tracey. Her voice had grown quiet again. Jackson thought she sounded almost scared.

"Hey, Jackson!" It was Oakley calling from the veranda.

"I've got to go now," Jackson said defiantly.

"Did he say what he was here for?" asked Tracey.

"He's been trying to talk to Prue. I suppose that's why he's been parking outside her house," Jackson said. "You tell her. I've got to practice." Tracey was silent.

"Hey," said Jackson, "do you want to come around and hear our band? It's wicked, man!"

"No," said Tracey. "I don't mix with enemies."

"Well, tell Tessa and the others," Jackson said. "Then you won't have to do all that signaling stuff. See you!"

He hung up, feeling braver than he had ever felt in his life, and ran out to the veranda where he sat himself down behind the drums. Happiness flooded over him.

"Party on!" he cried. He saw that Kester was laughing at him, but he didn't care. The music began again.

CHAPTER 11

In front of the veranda late-afternoon sunshine fell through the oak trees. Mrs. Flangrove began setting out plates on an outdoor table. Apparently the Flangroves were expecting friends for a summer barbecue under the trees. Mrs. Flangrove brought out fish steaks wrapped in tinfoil, and a trayful of hot dogs, and Sy Kennedy helped her to carry chairs out under the trees. The Barbie-Doll Club immediately sat down on the chairs, shaking their dolls at one another and talking in squeaky voices.

Suddenly, out by the gate, a movement caught Jackson's eye. He looked again and saw his cousin, Pete, walking by in an odd, slumped way, swinging a lumpy bag. A moment later it was Lorelei who passed the Flangroves' gateway, skipping in a jerky fashion like a windup doll. Jackson drummed enthusiastically, but he kept one eye on the gate. Sure enough, Tessa appeared next. Her head was jerking in all directions, just as if she were watching mosquitoes in the air around her. As Jackson watched her, she stopped, then waved one arm as if she was signaling to someone on a far hillside.

"Let's try the second piece again," said Portia. Jackson was happy to do this. He liked the thought that his Fortune cousins might be looking through the hedge and seeing his glory.

"A-one! A-two! A-one two three four!" counted Kester.

And Jackson crouched over his drums, drumming up a storm.

But suddenly Oakley's guitar stumbled and fell silent. So did Kester's. So did Portia's. Jackson was left drumming madly on his own.

"There's your sister," Oakley said.

"I know. She's always hanging out with the rest of the Barbie-doll freaks," said Jackson.

"Not that one. The other one," said Oakley. "Over there! It's Trace the Ace." He pointed to a gate in the opposite direction to the one Jackson was watching.

Jackson leapt to his feet, then sat down again, only it was more like falling down than actually sitting.

There was Tracey, standing where the path under the oak trees branched, looking around for him. She was wearing a tracksuit of Tessa's that was much too short in the arms and legs. Prue must have brought her, because Prue was there, too, wearing one of her weird hats and carrying Janey, who was grabbing at the gold tassels hanging around the hat's brim. Seeing Tracey and Prue walking in from one side, Tessa, Pete, and Lorelei crowded in through the gate on the Candle Lane side of the Flangroves' garden.

"The whole of your family seems to be coming," said Kester, sounding alarmed. "We'll need a thousand hot dogs."

"Tracey's come to *get* me," groaned Jackson. "Hide me!" He crouched down behind the drums.

But neither Tracey nor Prue was looking for Jackson. They seemed to be more interested in the grown-ups under the tree. Sy Kennedy must have felt them watching him. As he turned and saw them standing there in the dappled light, the late sunshine was reflected from the painted sun on his blue T-shirt. A sudden hush fell over the garden. Even the evening birds seemed to stop singing.

"That T-shirt looks as if Prue painted it," Jackson heard Leeanne saying.

Prue took a step toward the picnic table. Sy vaulted easily over a garden seat and ran toward her.

"Sy!" Jackson heard Prue say, the word sounding exactly like a sigh. She certainly wasn't angry.

"What's going on?" asked Oakley.

"Don't *talk* so loud," hissed Jackson. "Tracey will see me."

"Something romantic's happening," said Portia, staring at Sy and Prue. "Love at first sight."

"At second sight!" said Kester. "That's Prue Kennedy. She's actually come to see Sy."

"She must be going to give her ring back," said Portia. "If he gave her a ring, that is. Mom says they were both utterly poor."

But Sy and Prue suddenly fell into each other's arms even though other people were watching them. Tracey turned away, really embarrassed, and immediately saw Jackson crouching behind the drums. She actually grinned, and then walked toward the band.

"Hi!" she said. "Great drums!"

"What's going on?" asked Oakley. "Are they just saying good-bye?"

"It doesn't look like good-bye to me," said Portia.

Jackson came slowly out from behind the drums, trying to look as if he had been fixing something, rather than hiding.

"Cans!" he said to Tracey. "We call them cans."

Tracey nodded at the Flangroves in a reasonably friendly way. She was in their garden, and Prue was still hugging Sy Kennedy. Tracey had to be polite to them.

"When you said that the motorcyclist was Sy Kennedy I suddenly thought that perhaps he'd been trying to talk to her," she said. She turned to look over at Tessa. "I never believed he was waiting outside your house to steal wedding presents," she said scornfully.

Tessa, Lorelei, and Pete took this as an invitation to join in, and came closer.

"I think that's why he came to visit us," said Kester. "Not to steal wedding presents . . . just to talk to Prue. But she wouldn't talk to him."

"She didn't even know he was here," said Tracey. "*We* think Aunt Marama might have known, but if she did, she didn't let on to Prue. Aunt Marama was mad at him for taking off to Australia, and she really wants Prue to marry Chris Moody and stay here in Fairfield."

"I can't make out why Sy didn't just march in and say 'Here I am!' " said Kester. "He's not a wimp. He's tattooed."

"Has he got any money?" asked Tracey.

The Flangroves and the Fortunes looked at each other.

"Not much," said Portia.

"Well, Prue says she thinks he might be embarrassed because she was going to marry someone rich . . . well, someone with a car who could afford a warm house," Tracey explained. She was looking as much at the Fortune cousins as at the Flangroves. Behind her Sy Kennedy and Prue were no longer embracing. They were both looking at Janey, who was staring at Sy with an indignant expression.

"Who told her he was here?" asked Portia.

"Jackson told me and I told her," said Tracey. "I sort of didn't *want* to tell her, but I *had* to. When I went around to talk to her about being a bridesmaid she was in the house on her own, and she had his photographs out on the table."

"Does this mean none of us will be brides-maids?" asked Tessa. "I've been having pins stuck into me for an hour, and all for nothing!"

"But people have to be sure they love each other," said Lorelei in a sentimental voice.

"Mom bought all that pink material and it's already been cut up." Tessa didn't sound disappointed, however.

Tracey shrugged. "I *had* to tell her," she repeated. "It wouldn't have been fair not to."

And right then, for some reason, Jackson suddenly felt that if all the big sisters in the world had stood in a line, she was the one he would have chosen. He felt proud of her, though he didn't quite know why.

Mrs. Flangrove came out of the kitchen and stopped at the sight of so many people.

"*More* visitors?" she said. "Do we need more hot dogs?"

"We're not staying for dinner," said Tracey. "We just brought Prue along."

"I'm glad Sy was here," said Mrs. Flangrove. "He was planning to go and visit an old school friend, but he lost the key of his motorcycle and hasn't been able to find the spare. It seemed like bad luck at the time, but perhaps it wasn't such bad luck after all!"

Pete and Tessa turned and stared at Lorelei, who went bright red, and rattled something in her pocket.

CHAPTER 12

It was another school morning. . . .

Jackson came dancing down the passage. As he did so he heard family voices drifting in from the kitchen.

"I saw Chris Moody's mother at the supermarket the other day," his mother was saying.

"Is she speaking to the Fortune family yet?" asked his father, Peter.

"I don't know. We just stood there, looking at each other, and then she gave a funny smile and shrugged, and I smiled and shrugged. I mean, what can you say?"

"Nothing," said Peter. "Prue said it all. She said she wasn't going to marry Chris, and then she set off for Auckland in her Volkswagen, with Simon Kennedy riding his Norton after her, and they were married all over again in clothes that Prue had painted especially for the occasion. No family, no band, no bridesmaids! What a mess!"

"Oh, well, apparently he's got work. They're renting a cottage, and she says it's rough but sunny."

Jackson had heard all this the day before from Tracey and Tessa. On the mantelpiece stood a card with a picture of Frankenstein's monster painted on it. A speech bubble swelled from its lips, and a bolt stuck out of his neck. "I've bolted away," the monster was saying in sprawling, careless letters. Inside the card was written, "Love to our only true bridesmaid . . . from Prue and Sy," and there was a scribbly picture of Tracey whizzing along on her skateboard, pieces of her dress flying off behind her as she brandished a bouquet of flowers.

The Labradoodle rushed through the kitchen and Leeanne came rushing after him, threatening him with one of her Barbie dolls. She had been eating breakfast in the porch, and the Labradoodle had stolen her piece of toast. She couldn't get her toast back, of course, but she wanted revenge.

As the dog ran past him, Jackson sat transfixed. *The Labradoodles*. That was a wonderful name for a

band. Of course, the Flangroves would have to agree, but somehow Jackson felt sure they would. He drummed on the table with a spoon.

"Listen to this band rehearse. It's the coolest band in the un-i-verse." Somehow when he said *un-i-verse* like this he thought it sounded wider and grander and more far-reaching than it ever sounded said in the proper way during science at school.

Tracey came into the kitchen. She was dressed in blue jeans and a black top, and she had actually brushed her hair hard and tied it back with an elastic band. First, she held Angel while her mother made tea for her father. Then she made the twins sit at the table and eat their cornflakes.

"Are you going to school now?" she asked Jackson.

"Yes," he said, slinging his backpack over his shoulders and then picking up his sunglasses. However, he did not mean to wear them this morning. He put them into the front pocket of his pack, in case he needed them later.

"You can come with me," she said, looking at him doubtfully, as if she wasn't sure he would want to.

"I was going to, anyway," said Jackson. Tracey

and he were still the same people they had always been, yet sometimes they went in different directions these days. For two weeks Jackson had taken off after school to play the drums at the Flangroves' place. The band was practicing a sensational item for their first gig at the school concert. They would blow "Greensleeves" and the recorder group right off the stage of the school auditorium. Things had changed, and the changing hadn't stopped. Even there in the ordinary Fortune kitchen Jackson could feel invisible changes going on in the air around him.

Later, he and Tracey stood on the steps staring down the familiar street.

"You can go in front if you like," Tracey said unexpectedly.

"Cool!" cried Jackson. "I'd love to."

He set off on his skateboard. Tracey, balancing dangerously, followed him. The sidewalk stretched ahead, empty as far as the Main Road corner.

"Watch out, world, here we come!" Jackson yelled. He meant it too. Tracey followed him, laughing.

The Labradoodle watched them go. Then, waving his tail three times like a dog magician, he walked back toward the green gate. With a great sigh he lay down in a patch of sunshine with his nose on his paws, waiting until the afternoon when, one by one, they would all come home again.

ABOUT THE AUTHOR

Margaret Mahy is an internationally acclaimed storyteller who has twice won the British Library Association's Carnegie Medal and has received the (London) *Observer* Teenage Fiction Award. She has also won the Esther Glen Award of the New Zealand Library Association five times. Of her teenage novels published in the United States, *The Changeover* was a Best Book of the American Library Association and was the International Board on Books for Young People Honor Book in 1986. *Memory* was a *School Library Journal* Best Book and a *Boston Globe/Horn Book* Honor Book. She has written more than fifty books for young readers, including *The Good Fortunes Gang, A Fortunate Name,* and *A Fortune Branches Out,* Books One, Two, and Three of The Cousins Quartet.